Say Hello
to the Superstars
of the Animal World!

Meet Siberian tigers in Minnesota . . . giraffes in Florida . . . a famous gorilla from Chicago . . . a white tiger and white alligators in New Orleans . . . pandas in Washington, D.C. . . . a white koala in San Diego . . . Oregon's first American-born elephant since 1918 . . . baby one-horned rhinos in San Francisco . . . a walrus from Brooklyn . . . snow leopards from the Bronx! Has America gone to the animals? You bet! Come see them all and more in this fun-filled, picture-packed tour of our country's greatest zoos!

Books by Daniel Cohen

GHOSTLY TERRORS
THE GREATEST MONSTERS IN THE WORLD
HORROR IN THE MOVIES
THE MONSTERS OF STAR TREK
MONSTERS YOU NEVER HEARD OF
REAL GHOSTS
THE RESTLESS DEAD
SCIENCE FICTION'S GREATEST MONSTERS
STRANGE AND AMAZING FACTS ABOUT STAR TREK
SUPERMONSTERS
THE WORLD'S MOST FAMOUS GHOSTS

Books by Daniel and Susan Cohen

HEROES OF THE CHALLENGER
ROCK VIDEO SUPERSTARS
WRESTLING SUPERSTARS
WRESTLING SUPERSTARS II
YOUNG AND FAMOUS: SPORTS' NEWEST SUPERSTARS

Available from ARCHWAY Paperbacks

ZOO SUPERSTARS

DANIEL AND SUSAN COHEN

A MINSTREL® BOOK

PUBLISHED BY POCKET BOOKS

New York   London   Toronto   Sydney   Tokyo

A MINSTREL PAPERBACK *ORIGINAL*

A Minstrel Book published by
POCKET BOOKS, a division of Simon & Schuster Inc.
1230 Avenue of the Americas, New York, NY 10020

ISBN: 0-671-66709-2

First Minstrel Books Printing May 1989

10 9 8 7 6 5 4 3 2 1

A MINSTREL BOOK and colophon are registered trademarks
of Simon & Schuster Inc.

Printed in the U.S.A.

CONTENTS

AT THE ZOO

Have you been to the zoo lately? Chances are pretty good that you have. A lot of people have been going to the zoo.

Zoos are more popular than ever. Each year, more people visit zoos than go to all the professional football, baseball and basketball games combined!

New zoos are being built. Old zoos are being modernized.

The whole idea of the zoo has changed a lot. At one time, not too many years ago, zoos were collections of caged animals. Every big zoo tried to have one or two examples of as many different kinds of strange and exotic animals as possible. New zoos don't even have cages. "Cage is a four-letter word," says the director of one of America's best zoos.

In new zoos, many animals roam large outdoor enclosures. Indoor exhibits have been created to look remarkably like jungles or deserts or seashores. Animals are no longer grouped only by type. That is, the lions and tigers are not always put in the same building—called "the Lion House." Lions may be part of an African exhibit, the tigers part of an exhibit of Asian animals.

Sea animals have become a popular part of many zoos. Dolphins can now swim and leap in zoos that are hundreds or thousands of miles from the ocean. Some animals, like bats, were never in zoos because they were only active in the dark. A sleeping bat wasn't much to look at. Now, new lighting techniques can fool bats and other nocturnal animals into thinking day is night. The bats are happy, and so is the zoogoer who can see them fly.

Some zoos specialize. Zoos near the ocean often feature sea animals like dolphins and whales. Zoos in the desert have mainly desert animals, while those in the north have cold-weather animals. Some zoos have become expert in keeping elephants, others have done exceptionally well with cheetahs or gorillas.

There's a lot more to a zoo than display. Zoos have become an important part of worldwide conservation efforts. The best hope for many rare and threatened animals is the zoo. Animals that have been bred in zoos have been returned to the wild. It's a trend that most zoo officials think will continue.

Zoos have become a big part of education. They teach us all about the beauty and importance of the natural world. Zoos are also vital for science. Scientists have been able to learn a great deal about how animals live by watching zoo animals. A few years ago, Dr. Jane Goodall, who is world famous for her lifelong studies of wild chimpanzees in Africa, visited zoos in America. She said that zoos are getting better every year. "It is very encouraging to see."

But when we go to the zoo, we don't always think about all the important things that today's zoos are doing. We go to see the animals. And some animals are a lot more fun to see than others.

Just as there are superstars in the worlds of entertainment and sports, there are also zoo superstars. Don't laugh—a superstar means a lot to a zoo. When the Audubon zoo in New Orleans got a rare and beautiful white tiger, attendance jumped 40 percent. When pandas from

China's pandas visiting Busch Gardens
© *Busch Gardens, Tampa.*

China toured United States zoos, people lined up for hours just to catch a glimpse of them. The best-known residents of the city of San Diego are its zoo's koalas. The superstars help pull in the crowds that pay the admissions that help support the zoo and everything it does.

Now, as they say on TV, let's meet some of the zoo superstars, "up close and personal."

1

Koalas

SAN DIEGO ZOO

On September 21, 1985, an amazing thing happened in the Koala House at California's famous San Diego Zoo. A baby koala poked his pink nose out of his mother's pouch. What's so amazing about that? After all, koalas, like their nearest relatives, kangaroos, are marsupials. Marsupials are mammals that carry their babies in a pouch. A koala climbs into its mother's pouch as soon as it's born and stays there several months until it has finished growing.

But even though it's an everyday thing for a baby koala to poke his nose out of his mother's pouch, it's a highly unusual thing for that nose to be pink instead of black.

Goolara and mother
© Zoological Society of San Diego, 1986. Photo by Ron Garrison.

Odd, too, was the color of the baby's fur. Normal fur color for a koala is silvery gray. This pink-nosed baby had fur of snowy white. White koalas are so rare that, as far as anyone knows, there's only one other in the whole world, and you'd have to go all the way to Australia's Lone Pine Sanctuary to see it.

But, then, most people have to go to Australia to see koalas anyway. They're very rare outside their native land. Nowadays, koalas are so widely protected, it's hard to believe that these adorable creatures were once hunted nearly to extinction. We Americans can be very proud that the United States was the first country in the world

Goolara
© *Zoological Society of San Diego, 1987. Photo by Ron Garrison.*

to bar the import of koala furs. That was back in the 1920s.

Because of his white fur, San Diego Zoo staff dubbed their special baby koala Goolara, which means moonlight in the language of the aborigines—the original inhabitants of Australia. Not only does Goolara have a white coat and pink nose, he has pink eyes and pink claws. His mouth turns up in what looks like a pink smile. All this pink and white means that Goolara is an albino.

An albino has no coloration in his skin. Goolara inherited albinism from his parents. They were both gray, but each parent carried the recessive gene for the condition. If Goolara ever becomes a parent, his children will carry the gene, too. But because the gene is recessive, Goolara's children will probably be gray like their grandparents, instead of white like their father.

Bright sunlight isn't good for albinos, and like all koalas, Goolara heads indoors when the temperature falls to sixty-eight degrees. That means that Goolara is only outside when the weather's perfect. Then, along with the zoo's other Queensland koalas, he takes a turn at being exhibited. You'll find him perched in a tree near a tall viewing bridge in the koala part of the zoo. As for weather, don't worry. There's lots of perfect weather in San Diego. The climate is the main reason the zoo is able to exhibit so many different kinds of animals in such dazzling outdoor settings. So, if you do get to the San Diego Zoo, you stand a good chance of seeing Goolara.

Most of the zoo's visitors think Goolara looks just like a teddy bear. Koalas have always reminded people of little bears, and for years koalas were actually called koala bears. Some people still call them koala bears today. It's a charming name, but of course koalas aren't bears at all. There's no such thing as a marsupial bear.

Goolara and mother
© *Zoological Society of San Diego, 1986. Photo by Ron Garrison.*

Why are koalas exhibited in trees? Because that's where they live. Koalas are very good at grasping branches. They're also very good at sleeping. A koala sleeps twenty hours a day and spends the rest of the day eating. If you think you know kids who are picky eaters, you've never met a koala. Koalas eat only fresh eucalyptus leaves. Koalas eat so many eucalyptus leaves they smell like cough drops! The word koala means "no drink" because the lovable creatures who cling to the branches of eucalyptus trees in their native Australia get all the moisture they need from the trees' leaves, as well as all the nourishment they need. It's hard to imagine a more limited diet.

It's the koala's diet that makes the animal so hard to keep in zoos. Fortunately, eucalyptus trees grow well in San Diego's dry Australia-like climate, and fresh-cut eucalyptus branches are delivered daily to the San Diego Zoo's Koala House.

Next to Goolara, one of the biggest koala superstars at the zoo is Pulyara. Pulyara means long-snouted rat. Before Pulyara was born in July 21, 1985, no member of the zoo staff had ever seen a newborn koala. That's because the animals are so amazingly tiny and undeveloped at birth they're hard to see. But a keeper just happened to notice a furless one-half-inch-long creature making its way toward its mother's pouch that July day. The keeper thought the baby koala looked like a miniature rodent, so she named it Pulyara.

Months later, when Pulyara emerged from the pouch of his mother, Velvet, he was undersized and hungry. Velvet and Pulyara were taken to the zoo hospital, where veterinarians learned that Velvet was very ill. Both koalas almost died. To save Pulyara, keepers fed him from a special baby bottle just right for marsupials.

Baby koalas must have someone to cling to. Even to weigh baby koalas, San Diego Zoo keepers put them on a big stuffed teddy bear, so they'll feel safe. Then koala and teddy are placed on a scale together. To keep Pulyara feeling safe, he was introduced to Jan, a female koala whose baby had died. Jan adopted Pulyara, and he was happy to ride around on her back koala-style for months.

Pulyara grew up to be a healthy koala. Velvet got well, too, and in 1987 she had another baby. The baby's father is Walt. Walt's name comes from the Australian song "WALTzin' Matilda." Walt is also a very special koala. He's the first koala in history to travel east of the Mississippi River.

At the age of nine, Walt was selected to spend a month at the Cincinnati, Ohio, Zoo. Movie stars usually travel with their hairdresser, secretary, and press agent in tow. Walt took his keeper along, instead. Movie stars usually fly luxury class. Walt boarded his plane in a glamorous traveling crate equipped with a tree. Movie stars take a lot of clothes along when they travel. Walt's luggage consisted of sixty pounds of eucalyptus leaves.

At the Cincinnati Airport, the marvelous marsupial entered a limousine and was given a motorcycle escort to the zoo. There, a crowd waited in line for hours for one glimpse of the 15-pound koala. Later, he appeared on a local talk show where, fortunately, his keeper was on hand to answer the questions. He was the guest of honor at a fabulous party, too. Despite arriving at the party in a Rolls Royce, Walt remained unspoiled. While the other guests sipped champagne, he quietly ate eucalyptus leaves and then took a nap.

Walt's visit started a trend. Since Cincinnati, other koalas from the San Diego Zoo have been exhibited at several major American zoos. Perhaps a koala will come your way soon. You'll know, because there'll be plenty of local publicity first. Still, the best place to see koalas in America is at the great San Diego Zoo.

If you want to visit the San Diego Zoo, here is the address:

The San Diego Zoo
Park Boulevard and Zoo Place
Balboa Park
San Diego, California 92112

2

Cheetahs

ST. LOUIS ZOO

Back in 1973, the staff of the St. Louis Zoo decided it was time to replace the old Lion House. The house had been used for all the big cats. The new outdoor exhibit was to be called Big Cat Country. It would feature lions, tigers, jaguars, pumas and leopards. But the zoo decided against putting cheetahs in the new exhibit.

While cheetahs are certainly big cats, they are different from the others. They don't roar, they only purr. The cheetah is the only cat that cannot retract its claws. Even your house cat can do that. Actually, young cheetahs can retract their claws. When they grow up, they lose that

Cheetahs
St. Louis Zoo photo by Steve Bircher.

ability. Most of all, cheetahs are shy and solitary. They don't like to be around other big cats. Lions and tigers make them nervous.

The zoo officials thought that the cheetahs should have a place of their own. As it happened, the bison had been moved, and the old bison yard was vacant. It was a nice quiet spot, west of the Elephant House. So the one-and-a-half-acre area was landscaped to resemble the cheetahs' African home. A new fence was put in. Cheetahs are not great climbers, but they are better climbers than bison, so they required a higher fence. A heated den was installed, and four cheetahs, two male and two female, were turned

Cheetahs
St. Louis Zoo photo.

loose in the yard. They took to their new home at once. Even though the cheetahs' new home was in a remote part of the zoo, people came to see it. They loved to see the graceful cats roaming with relative freedom. It soon became one of the St. Louis Zoo's most popular exhibits.

Showing off the cheetahs is just part of the purpose of this exhibit. Like many other large animals, the cheetahs in the world are growing fewer in number. They have been hunted, and some of the places where they live have been turned into farmland. But the number of cheetahs in the world seems to have been going down for a long time. No one really knows why.

Since cheetahs are not nearly as ferocious as lions and tigers, they have been kept as pets and hunting animals for thousands of years. The pharaohs of Egypt trained cheetahs for hunting. So did Roman emperors. The Emperor of China is said to have had hundreds of trained cheetahs. Just in case you're thinking of getting one for a pet, you had better forget it. When full grown, a cheetah will weigh over 100 pounds. Even though they have pretty good tempers, they still have big teeth, and can be extremely dangerous if they become angry or frightened. They may have been fine for an emperor's palace. But they will not fit comfortably into a modern apartment.

Even though people have been keeping cheetahs for a long time, they have very rarely been able to breed them. Lions and tigers breed easily in captivity, though they are much wilder animals. Cheetahs do not. Once again, no one really knows why.

The St. Louis Zoo keepers decided that they would make cheetahs their special project. The new exhibit was named the Cheetah Survival Center. The aim was to breed cheetahs. Have they been successful? You bet they have. In 1976, the zoo got two captive-born cheetahs from another zoo. The first litter of cheetahs at the St. Louis Zoo was born in 1973. Since that time, there have been more than twenty cheetah cubs born at the Cheetah Survival Center. No other zoo in America can match that record. St. Louis, Missouri, is a long way from the African plains where the cheetahs come from. But the sleek and graceful animals are getting along better on the banks of the Mississippi than practically anywhere else in the world. Currently, there are eight cheetahs at the zoo, and five more are on loan to other zoos.

Cheetahs are secretive and rather mysterious animals. People have been observing them in zoos and in the wild

Cheetahs
St. Louis Zoo photo.

for a long time. But there is still a great deal that we don't know about their habits. The St. Louis Zoo's Cheetah Survival Center is helping us learn a lot more about them.

One thing that everyone knows about cheetahs is that they're fast—generally believed to be the fastest animals in the world. Over short distances, they can sprint up to sixty miles an hour. Long and slender, they're built for speed.

Cheetahs are good-looking. They have a yellow or tan coat with black spots. They also have black spots or patches on the backs of their ears. Some zoologists think that these ear spots serve as fake eyes. If an enemy approaches a cheetah from behind and sees the black spots, it may think that they are real eyes, and that the cheetah is looking right at him.

Like so many of today's zoos, the St. Louis Zoo is not only a great place to go and look at animals, but also a place that is helping to preserve some of the world's most wonderful animals.

Of course, there is much more than the Cheetah Survival Center to see at the St. Louis Zoo. The zoo is particularly proud of its new Jungle of the Apes building. There, gorillas, orangutans and chimpanzees live in large enclosures that duplicate their rain-forest homes. Just outside the spectacular building is a larger-than-life-size statue of one of the St. Louis Zoo's superstars of the past, Phil, a gorilla who was a great favorite with visitors for seventeen years.

If you want to visit or write the St. Louis Zoo, the address is:

St. Louis Zoological Park
Forest Park
St. Louis, Missouri 63110

3

Elephants

WASHINGTON PARK ZOO

When Packy the elephant was born at the Washington Park Zoo, in Portland, Oregon, on April 14, 1962, the city went wild. The birth of the two-hundred-twenty-five-pound baby elephant was shown live on Portland television. Packy's birth was big news outside Portland, too. Newspapers around the world trumpeted his arrival. Why all the fuss? Because Packy's birth was a historic event. Not since 1918 had an elephant been born in the United States.

There are two kinds of elephants, Asian and African. Packy's an Asian elephant. He still lives at the Washington Park Zoo along with eleven other Asian elephants.

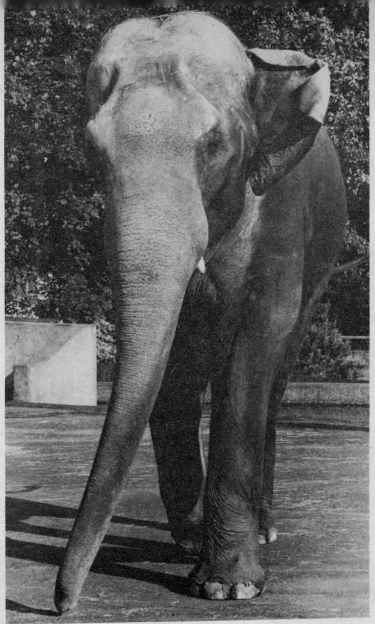

Packy
Washington Park Zoo, Portland, Oregon. Photo by Jesse Karr.

Chang Dee
Washington Park Zoo, Portland, Oregon. Photo by Jesse Karr.

African elephants have huge ears, big tusks, high shoulders with a hollow in midback, and their trunks end in two fingerlike tips. Compared to African elephants, Asian elephants have small ears and small tusks. They are smaller in size than African elephants. That doesn't mean Packy is small. He stands ten feet high at the shoulder and weighs over 12,000 pounds.

Packy's trunk, like the trunks of all Asian elephants, ends in a single fingerlike tip. A trunk is really a very long nose. Packy's trunk is for breathing and smelling. He can also suck up water into his trunk and pick up food with it. He can use it to carry a heavy log or to carry a tiny peanut. Speaking of peanuts, giant-size Packy can really pack away lots of food. Want to know what he eats? Every day, Packy devours one fifty-pound box of carrots, one to two boxes of lettuce, one gallon of oats, one gallon of special zoo pellets made up of vitamins and iron tablets, and one to two bales of hay.

Elephants in the wild get plenty of exercise searching for food. In zoos, elephants often become fat and lazy. To keep Packy and the other elephants in shape, the Washington Park Zoo has an exercise machine. The machine tosses apples around in all directions. Few elephants can resist apples, even when they have to move around to pick them up. Training elephants to perform tricks is another way to see that the animals get enough exercise. Elephants are intelligent, learn tricks quickly, and enjoy showing off. No wonder they're superstars at circuses as well as at zoos.

The exercise machine is just one of the things that makes the elephant facility at the Washington Park Zoo special. There's also a bubbling pool and a large sand-covered yard. The bubbling pool is good for the elephant's feet. Sand is great for elephants' feet. The rooms inside

Chang Dee
Washington Park Zoo, Portland, Oregon. Photo by Jesse Karr.

the elephant barn are heated and have remote controlled doors. The remote-controlled doors are very important. No matter how friendly an elephant is, any animal that weighs thousands of pounds can be dangerous. Zoos make sure that the people who come to see the animals are safe. The problem is protecting zoo keepers and zoo veterinarians.

As they age, male elephants often become very grouchy. That's why many zoos keep only females and young males. But a zoo cannot run a successful breeding program without mature males. Thanks to remote-controlled doors, the Washington Park Zoo has solved that problem. If a male elephant's in a bad mood, he can move freely from one room to another without meeting his keeper face to face.

But if keepers can keep away from elephants part of the time, what about veterinarians? A veterinarian can't examine a sick elephant if the elephant's locked in the next room. The vet must get up close. The answer is a set of movable, remote-controlled, steel-bar walls called a "squeezer." A squeezer doesn't really squeeze an elephant. It pens the elephant in, so that the veterinarian can safely examine and treat the enormous animal.

A few months after Packy was born, a female elephant named Me-Tu was born at the Washington Park Zoo. The births brought the zoo the 1962 Edward H. Bean Award. The Bean award is given by the American Association of Zoological Parks and Aquariums in honor of the most important birth or hatching in a United States zoo.

The elephant birth rate at the Washington Park Zoo has continued to skyrocket. In the past thirteen years, Packy himself has fathered seven babies. The people of Portland are proud that more elephants have been born at their zoo than at any other zoo in the world. Good thing, too! The number of elephants in Asia keeps shrinking, and no Asian country will allow elephants to leave home anymore. So, if it wasn't for the elephants born at the Washington Park Zoo, the day might come when there were no elephants left in the United States. Imagine going to a zoo and not finding a single elephant. That would be galumphing awful. Fortunately, the Washington Park Zoo has sent several baby elephants to other zoos, and its own herd keeps growing. The herd is doing so well the zoo now sells elephant fertilizer. Called Zoodoo, the fertilizer is a hit with gardeners throughout the Portland area.

Though Packy remains the superstar of the Washington Park Zoo, these days he has to share the spotlight with an adorable baby elephant named Chang Dee. Born in May, 1987, Chang Dee is Me-Tu's latest baby. It's not surprising that the friendly Chang Dee is a real crowd pleaser. His father, Hugo, used to be with the circus. Chang Dee will soon be following in his father's footsteps by joining the circus, too.

1987 not only saw the birth of Chang Dee, it was a big year for Packy. He turned twenty-five. The zoo threw Packy a super birthday party. Packy ate a forty-pound whole-wheat birthday cake frosted with peanut butter, while a high school band played "Happy Birthday." A flock of human visitors was on hand to celebrate. Many signed the giant elephant's birthday card.

Elephants live a long time, maybe even as long as seventy years. If you like elephants, wish Packy many more happy birthdays to come.

If you want to visit the Washington Park Zoo, here's the address:

Washington Park Zoo
4001 S. W. Canyon Road
Portland, Oregon 97221

4

Pandas

THE NATIONAL ZOO

Some call it panda-mania. Others call it panda-monium. Whatever you call the giant panda craze, one thing is clear. Pandas are the number one zoo superstars in the world. One look at a panda, and you'll see why. With their round faces, stick-up ears, licorice eyes, eye patches, and furry bodies, they look like big black-and-white stuffed toys.

But it isn't easy to find a panda to look at. The panda is one of the most endangered species on earth. Fewer than a thousand pandas are left in the wild, and there are very few pandas in zoos. Pandas are full-time permanent residents at one place only in the entire United States. That's the National Zoo in Washington, D.C. Since 1972, the National Zoo has been home to a male panda named Hsing-Hsing and a female panda named Ling-Ling. The National Zoo is a not-to-be-missed-no-matter-what stop for any family visiting the nation's capital, and the panda exhibit is a not-to-be-missed-no-matter-what stop at the zoo.

Arrive at the zoo at the right moment, and you might be lucky enough to see a panda waddle over to the jungle gym in the panda yard. The jungle gym has ramps a panda can climb, a tunnel for pandas to crawl through, and a deck where pandas can relax, nap, or munch on bamboo. Pandas love bamboo.

A long movable wrist bone that works like a stubby thumb makes it possible for pandas to grasp their food human-style. A panda eats sitting up or half lying on his back. He holds a bamboo stalk in his forepaw and, with his broad teeth and powerful jaws, crushes the tough bamboo. He eats practically every bit of the plant: stalk, leaves and shoots. In the wild, a panda will eat herbs, flowers, small animals, corn and honey when he can find such food. In zoos, besides bamboo, pandas eat liver, eggs, fresh vegetables, cornmeal, rice, powdered milk and yogurt.

Hsing-Hsing and Ling-Ling's jungle gym was built by a group of children and adults who are members of FONZ, Friends of the National Zoo. Volunteers from FONZ also take turns panda watching. Their job is to keep close track of a panda's daily activities. A panda's day is also caught on videotape. Why all the panda watching and videotaping? If pandas are to be saved from extinction, scientists must learn all they can about the animals. There's plenty left to learn. Experts still don't know exactly what pandas are. They look like bears and walk like

Washington's panda
Jessie Cohen, Office of Graphics and Exhibits, National Zoological Park.

Yong Yong at Busch Gardens
© *Busch Gardens, Tampa*

bears, but they don't hibernate. Their teeth, diet, and fur-color pattern would seem to put them in the raccoon family. But some experts think pandas are really in a class by themselves.

Panda watchers may do the observing at the National Zoo, but a team of special panda keepers sees to it that the black-and-white creatures have everything they need. The first thing a panda keeper learns is that, while pandas may look like stuffed toys, they're not. They're big, strong animals. Though a newborn panda is a tiny thing measuring only a few inches in length and weighing as little as five ounces, a full-grown panda measures five to six feet in length and can weigh as much as 300 pounds. Just try cuddling 300 pounds of animal if that animal wants to be left alone. Most of the time, pandas do want to be left alone. In the wild, a panda keeps to himself. He likes to keep to himself in a zoo, too.

Shortly after Ling-Ling arrived at the National Zoo, she cornered one of her keepers in her enclosure. Ling-Ling tried to bite the keeper's right leg, but luckily she just chewed through the top of his boot. To keep Ling-Ling from gnawing on his left boot, the keeper kept kicking his left leg in the air. Ling-Ling was so cute that zoo visitors watching these antics through a thick wall of glass thought the keeper was dancing with the panda. Finally, someone realized what was happening and called for help. The keeper was rescued.

Pandas make their home in China, and in 1987, China sent several pandas to the United States and Canada on loan. Two of the well-traveled pandas, Ling-Ling and Yong-Yong, stayed for months at a time in different zoos. Unlike the National Zoo's Ling-Ling, this Ling-Ling was a male. Yong-Yong was a female. This Ling-Ling was born in the Beijing, China, Zoo, and Yong-Yong was brought there after being abandoned in the wild as a baby. Isn't it great that someone found her?

The first live panda ever to reach the United States was the very first live panda ever to leave China. He was a baby panda named Su-Lin who moved into Chicago's Brookfield Zoo in 1936. Before 1865, no one from Europe or America had ever seen a panda. That's because pandas live in a harsh, faraway part of China. For centuries, few people chose to live there or go there, and the rare panda was rarely seen.

Pandas don't mind their harsh environment. Because they're shy animals who need shade, high tree-covered mountain forests suit them. The thick bamboo stands in the panda's natural habitat make tough going for people, but thanks to their strong, powerful legs and padded feet, pandas move through them with ease. They don't mind cold, either. Their coarse, thick coats keep them warm. Snow certainly doesn't bother pandas. In the wild, a young panda will play in the snow. Turning himself into a panda sled, he'll lie down in a clearing and slide downhill.

Because China is a very crowded country, people have finally moved into the areas where pandas live. They cut down the bambo pandas eat and the trees that protect them. This loss of habitat is one of the main reasons why pandas are almost extinct. The other reason is that the bamboo that pandas eat flowers and dies every fifty to one hundred years. The bamboo does grow back, but slowly. That means for years at a time pandas can't find enough food.

What is being done to save the panda? The Chinese love their pandas very much, and even though it's a hardship in such a poor, crowded country, they have set aside twelve panda preserves. They've also planted bamboo. With the aid of many other countries, including the

United States, China has set up panda breeding stations in the preserves (nicknamed panda-miniums). Some pandas have been born at these breeding stations and in Chinese zoos. A few pandas have been born outside China, but no panda born in the United States has survived.

The panda craze has made pandas the royal family of the animal kingdom. So, let's hope the day comes when every major zoo has a panda exhibit and many pandas are born in the wild. Wouldn't that be panda-perfect?

If you want to visit the National Zoo, here is the address:

National Zoological Park
3000 Block of Connecticut Avenue, N.W.
Washington, D.C. 20008

5

Siberian Tigers

MINNESOTA ZOO

It gets cold and snowy around Minneapolis, Minnesota, during the winter. The Minnesota Zoo, which is located just south of the twin cities of Minneapolis and St. Paul, is like most zoos; it has animals from all over the world. You can see tropical birds, and pythons from India, all displayed in the most naturalistic setting possible. The tropics are inside a well-heated building.

What really makes this zoo special, one of America's best zoos, is its collection of cold-weather animals. Visitors strolling along the part of the zoo called the Northern Trail can see musk ox and bison, wild horses from Mongolia, and two-humped camels from the frigid des-

Siberian tiger
Minnesota Zoological Garden. Photo by T. Cajacob.

Siberian tiger and cub
Minnesota Zoological Garden. Photo by T. Cajacob.

erts of northern Asia. There are wolves and arctic foxes and tigers. Wait a minute, you say. Tigers live in the jungle. They can't live outside in Minnesota where temperatures often drop to thirty degrees below zero. True enough, some kinds of tigers do come from the steaming jungles. They have to be kept in heated buildings in such a climate. But the biggest and most magnificent of all the world's tigers is the Siberian tiger. This giant cat finds the Minnesota winter just fine; in fact, a bit warmer than it was back in Siberia.

During the summertime, Siberian tigers try to find ways to cool off. Their exhibit has a waterfall and several pools. Visitors are often surprised to see the tigers swimming or just resting in the water. Cats are not supposed to like water. Most don't, but tigers are different. They are good swimmers, and they enjoy it. In the winter, tiger cubs can be seen frolicking in the snow, even on the coldest days.

There are several varieties of tiger, all a little different. The Siberian is the giant. These tigers may grow to sixteen feet, from tip of nose to tip of tail, and weigh up to 650 pounds. They are slightly lighter in color than their cousins to the south. But in all other respects, they are the same as the more familiar Bengal tiger.

The Siberian tiger is one of the rarest of all the varieties of tiger, and the Minnesota Zoo specializes in them. There are usually seven or eight, including cubs, on display at one time. Other Minnesota tigers are on loan to other zoos around the country.

Like many of the other animals we have talked about in this book, the Siberian tiger has been pushed out of many of the places where it once lived. In the wild, there is a threat to its survival. But fortunately, these animals do very well in zoos. In fact, it's sometimes hard to find zoos that need or want more tiger cubs.

Minnesota Zoo officials want to make sure that there will be a healthy population of tigers in zoos for hundreds of years. But they don't want to just keep them in zoos. As people's ideas about animals and of land change, the zoo workers hope that large areas will be set aside for tigers and other threatened animals. Then, animals that had lived for generations in zoos could go back to their original homes. In the meantime, it's the job of the zoos to keep their captive tigers healthy and happy, and to provide a place for people to see them.

The Siberian tigers do not spend their nights outside. That probably wouldn't be safe. They are taken inside every night to be fed. What does a Siberian tiger eat? At Minnesota, it's a specially prepared meat-based diet. It's a bit like some of the canned food you feed your pet cat. An adult male will eat about eight to ten pounds of this diet every day. Females are a little smaller, so they eat a little less.

Every two years, each tiger gets a complete physical and dental examination. Tigers are given bones to chew in order to keep their teeth and gums in good shape. Still, dental problems are common. Tigers don't make regular visits to the dentist, but a dentist does make a regular trip to the tigers. Cleaning a tiger's teeth is a tricky business, and the tigers have to be tranquilized. Tiger cubs are cute and playful. Adult tigers are magnificent looking, but they aren't playful anymore. No dentist wants to put his hand into the mouth of a fully awake tiger.

The Minnesota Zoo has other cold-weather animals that are worth seeing. There is an exhibit of moose. The moose is not a rare or exotic animal, but have you ever seen a moose in a zoo? Probably not. They are hard to keep in zoos, and only a handful have them.

Then there is the Japanese macaque—that's a kind of

monkey. There may be cold-weather tigers, you say, but there certainly can't be cold-weather monkeys. Yet, that's exactly what the Japanese macaque is. They come from the cold northern parts of Japan. Sometimes, they have been called snow monkeys. The zoo has a troop of these unusual monkeys. They can often be seen outside, braving the Minnesota snow.

Then there are reindeer—yes, there really are such animals as reindeer. The reindeer is actually a domestic animal for people who live in some far northern regions. W. Clement Moore, who wrote the poem popularly called "The Night Before Christmas," was the first one to make a connection between Santa Claus and reindeer. Then came the Christmas song "Rudolph, the Red-Nosed Reindeer." It's now hard to imagine Santa without his reindeer. No one in America can think about reindeer without thinking about Christmas.

The Minnesota Zoo got its first two reindeer in 1984. The keepers decided to teach the reindeer to pull a sleigh. That's what they do where they come from. It takes special training to get them to pull. One of the keepers who had trained horses figured that training reindeer would be about the same. It wasn't. The reindeer have entirely different personalities. Besides, the harness kept getting tangled in their antlers. Finally, after many hours of hard and frustrating work, the reindeer did learn to pull a sleigh.

Now, the Minnesota Zoo reindeer are a regular part of the holiday season. They are in demand for parades and personal appearances. They are shown in all sorts of Christmas advertising. And at Christmastime, zoo visitors line up to have their pictures taken with Santa and a couple of his very real reindeer.

There's another thing unique about this northern zoo—

it may be the only zoo in the world where visitors can view the exhibits while skiing. During the winter, the Minnesota Zoo opens several cross-country ski trails that go past many of the major outdoor exhibits of cold-weather animals. And after skiing, you can warm up in the tropics. At the zoo, they're only a few steps away. Here is the address:

The Minnesota Zoo
12101 Johnny Cake Ridge Road
Apple Valley, Minnesota 55124

6

Orangutan

PHILADELPHIA ZOO

On April 18, 1987, the Philadelphia, Pennsylvania, Airport was packed with reporters and television crews. The media were there to greet a flight from Phoenix, Arizona. When the plane landed, a superstar got off, and the camera crews and reporters went bananas. Was the superstar an NFL linebacker? A member of a rock band? No, better yet, he was a fifteen-year-old orangutan named Bim. At 250 pounds, Bim weighs as much as a football player, and compared to Bim, even the most exotic rock star looks quite ordinary. Bim is four-and-a-half feet tall. He has an orange face, and his body is covered with orange hair. He has very long arms. A large pouch hangs below his chin, and fleshy pads grow from the sides of his face.

Bim
Photo by James Jones, courtesy Philadelphia Zoo.

Once finished with the media, Bim was taken from the airport to the Philadelphia Zoo, where he spent ninety days in quarantine. When the zoo staff was sure he was in good health, he was moved into the zoo's primate center, which is a wonderful place for an ape to live. There, Bim was given a box, a ball, and a barrel to play with, but these things just bored him. Then, a keeper gave him a nice new wool blanket. Like Linus in the Peanuts comic strip, Bim really took to his blanket. The blanket made Bim more popular than ever, and people came to the zoo in huge numbers just to take his picture.

Outside on a warm day, Bim would spread his blanket on the ground. On cool days, he would cover himself with the blanket or wrap it around his head like a hood.

37

Finally, he tore the blanket in two and started wearing half of it wrapped around his throat like a scarf. He wore the other half around his feet. An orangutan wearing a blanket is quite a sight. If you know anyone who is grumpy, send that person to the Philadelphia Zoo to see Bim. Bim can make anyone smile.

Orangutans come from Borneo and Sumatra, which are islands in the East Indies. Bim is a Bornean orangutan. He was born in the Phoenix Zoo, but his mother and father were brought to Phoenix from Borneo. The word orangutan means "man of the forest." Apes have always seemed very human to people, and apes and people do have a lot in common. So the word fits. As for the forest part of the word, it describes the animal well, too. In the wild, orangutans live in trees.

When it's time to sleep, orangutans sleep in the trees. They build sleeping platforms for themselves out of branches. When an orangutan wants to travel, he swings slowly from tree limb to tree limb. Zoos know how important trees are to orangutans, and you'll usually find trees or tree forms in the orangutan exhibit. At the Philadelphia Zoo, orangutans live in a lush natural setting that makes them feel right at home.

Since Bim is such a delightful animal, you probably want to know why the Phoenix Zoo sent him to Philadelphia. He's there as part of an orangutan breeding program. Someday, he may go back to Phoenix. If he does, many of his human fans will probably be at the airport when his plane leaves to say goodbye.

Visitors to the Philadelphia Zoo have plenty to see after they've finished watching orangutans. The zoo has been making zoo news since the day it was chartered. That was in 1854, which makes the Philadelphia Zoo the oldest zoo in the United States. The zoo is so proud of being America's first zoo, it has named its zoo publication, *Zoo One*. Older Philadelphians, whose great-great-grandparents took them to see the zoo when they were children, are now taking their great-great-grandchildren to the same zoo to see the animals. Of course, the zoo has changed over the years, and there are lots of new exhibits.

One of the most popular exhibits is Bear Country, where polar bears dive off twelve-foot cliffs. Visitors can get within inches of the bears as they swim in their 200,000-gallon swimming pool.

Then, there's the Rare Animal House. Among the unusual animals, you'll see there are a giant squirrel (measuring one full yard from the tip of his nose to the tip of his tail) and a colorful bird called a hornbill. The bird has a huge beak. A tortoise with a soft flat shell and a gray monkey whose babies are born with yellow, orange, or reddish fur are also star attractions of the Rare Animal House.

Kids can climb a pretend giant beehive, hatch from a make-believe egg, or even ride a dinosaur at the zoo's Treehouse facility. The Children's Zoo makes a great setting for birthday parties. Kids get dinner, ice cream, party hats, souvenirs, and a sea lion show. Actually, any part of the zoo or even the whole zoo can be reserved for a party. Some Philadelphians love their zoo so much they've gotten married there! Maybe next time you have a birthday party, you'll hold it at the Philadelphia Zoo and invite Bim.

If you want to visit the Philadelphia Zoo, here is the address:

The Zoological Society of Philadelphia
34th Street and Girard Avenue
Philadelphia, Pennsylvania 19104

7

Giraffes
BUSCH GARDENS

When a reticulated giraffe was born at Busch Gardens in Tampa, Florida, recently, the zoo sent out a birth announcement. The announcement sounded like an April Fool's Day joke. The newborn infant was described as weighing eighty-five pounds. Its height? Six feet. It's hard to believe a baby anything could measure six feet long at birth. But the Busch Gardens birth announcement was telling the truth. Giraffes really are born six feet tall. Giraffes are the tallest mammals on earth. They grow to a height of eighteen feet. An adult animal can weigh over a ton. If giraffes were athletes, the Busch Gardens tall slender baby would be headed toward stardom in the NBA.

Giraffes
Busch Gardens, Tampa.

Giraffe feeding time.
Busch Gardens, Tampa.

If you're wondering what the word "reticulated" means, it means network. Reticulated giraffes are covered by a network of narrow creamy lines that enclose a pattern of copper-colored splotches. Thanks to its coloration and its soft velvety eyes, the reticulated giraffe is very beautiful. But like all giraffes, it's also an amazing and comical sight, thanks to its very, very long neck, its long thin legs, and its astonishing seventeen-inch-long tongue. All giraffes have short horns on the head and a short stiff mane of hair running along the neck.

42

Reticulated giraffes are native to Kenya in East Africa. There, the animals live in herds. Giraffes don't like deep forests. They like open land dotted with trees. Living in the open can be dangerous for animals, but giraffes are far from helpless. They have good eyes, so they can spot trouble fast. Good runners, giraffes can get away from trouble quickly, too. If push comes to shove, they have a very strong kick. Even a lion would rather not be kicked by a giraffe.

In the wild, giraffes eat mainly the leaves and twigs of the spiny acacia tree. Their long necks give them the edge over other animals in browsing. While shorter animals must compete for food nearer the ground, the tall giraffe is free to nibble away at leaves and branches no one else can reach. Unlike some animals, such as koalas, giraffes adjust easily to a change in diet. This makes it a lot easier to keep giraffes in zoos. At Busch Gardens, you'll find giraffes cheerfully chomping on alfalfa hay.

One thing you won't find giraffes doing is making a lot of noise. Giraffes don't shriek, roar, bellow, squeak, bark or croak. The animals are so quiet that for many years people thought they were voiceless. But after studying giraffes closely, experts learned that the animals do make whistling and gurgling noises, though not very often.

Busch Gardens, The Dark Continent—as the family entertainment center and zoo is officially called—is a wonderful place to see giraffes. The striking looking animals roam freely at the Africa-themed park's Serengeti Plain exhibit. A new herd brought over from Africa joined the park's original herd in 1984.

Back in 1965, Busch Gardens was one of the first zoos in the United States to turn zoodom upside down by "caging" people instead of animals. Cages for people come in the form of monorail cars, skyrides, and trains, while the animals are given the run of many acres. Busch Gardens visitors get a safe close-up view of animals living as they would in their natural habitat. The animals are safe, too, from each other. A deep moat keeps lions away from zebras and giraffes.

Serengeti Plain zoo attendants try to keep their distance from the exhibit's inhabitants, so the animals can lead as human-free a life as possible. It's the attendants' job to keep count of the animals, inoculate newborn babies, keep an eye out for sick animals who may need a trip to the zoo's hospital, and deliver truckloads of food. Food delivery is the part of the attendants' job the animals like best.

The list of what to see at the award-winning Busch Gardens zoo is as long as a giraffe's neck. Look for flamingos in the bird exhibit. Peek through the windows of the animal nursery. Check out the terrific summer zoo camp for kids.

If you want to visit Busch Gardens, here is the address:

Busch Gardens, The Dark Continent
3000 Busch Boulevard
Tampa, Florida 33674

8

Gorillas

BROOKFIELD ZOO

You have probably seen the famous film *King Kong.* King Kong is supposed to be a gigantic gorilla, and a monster. True, he is a monster we can love and feel sorry for, but he is very definitely a monster—huge, fierce and wild. The film was made more than fifty years ago. At the time, a lot of people really thought gorillas were fierce and wild animals. Now, we know differently.

The gorilla is one of the most gentle and peaceable animals on earth. If left alone, it will spend all its time eating and sleeping, and never bother anyone. Of course, a gorilla is large and very strong. When defending itself, it

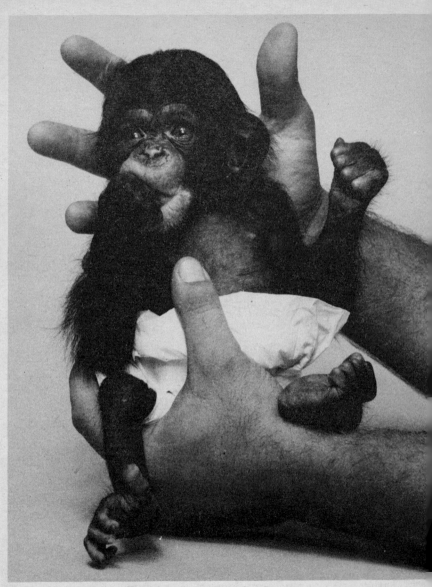

Mark, a baby chimpanzee at Busch Gardens.
Busch Gardens, Tampa.

can be dangerous. But even the famous displays of ferocity, the bellowing and chest beating, are mainly bluff. Despite their size and reputation, they are truly lovable animals.

Whenever a gorilla appears in a zoo, it becomes an immediate favorite. So, when Samson, a large male gorilla, arrived at Chicago's Brookfield Zoo, he was expected to be a big hit, and he was. Samson is what is called a silverback male. The fur of most gorillas is entirely black. However, as they get older and bigger, male gorillas will develop a large silvery patch of hair on their backs—that's why they are called silverbacked.

Samson was born in the West African jungle in 1961. He actually belongs to the zoo in Buffalo, New York, but he is on long-term loan to Brookfield. Zoos regularly lend animals to one another for various reasons. The reason Samson was lent to Brookfield was that the zoo has several female gorillas. Zoos are very anxious to breed gorillas. Samson has fathered several offspring since he came to Brookfield.

Because they are so easygoing, gorillas do quite well in zoos. They live up to fifty years. The biggest problem for zoo gorillas is that they get fat and lazy. In the wild, they have to spend a lot of time moving around, looking for enough fruit and other vegetable matter to eat. In the zoo, a tasty collection of apples, oranges, bananas, grapes, raisins, sweet potatoes, carrots, celery, onions, green beans, lettuce, spinach and kale is presented to them twice a day. At Brookfield, each gorilla also gets a cup of yogurt daily.

After that kind of a meal, the gorilla doesn't have to move at all. In the old days, when gorillas were in cages, they didn't. But Samson and the other Brookfield Zoo gorillas don't live in cages. They roam the largest indoor

Samson
© 1985 Chicago Zoological Society. Photo by Mike Greer.

Samson
© 1984 Chicago Zoological Society. Photo by Mike Greer.

gorilla exhibit in the world. It's set up to look like their jungle home. There's plenty to look at, plenty to climb on and explore, plenty to keep them busy and interested. That helps them keep their figures trim.

While Samson and the other gorillas probably attract more attention than any other animal at the zoo, the reigning queen of Brookfield Zoo is Olga. She's not a gorilla, she's a walrus. Olga came to Brookfield in 1961 when she was about six months old. Right now, she is the oldest walrus in any zoo.

Olga dines royally on seafood, downing from forty to sixty pounds of squid, clams and mackerel a day. That

Olga the walrus waves to her fans.
© *1986 Chicago Zoological Society*

sounds like a lot until you realize that Olga herself weighs 2,000 pounds. She costs about $15,000 a year to feed, making her the most expensive animal in the zoo to feed. But she's well worth the price. She's a Chicago celebrity.

In 1987, when the one-ton walrus was moved from her old pool to a brand-new exhibit, it became a real media event in Chicago. Zoo public relations people billed the move as "the big splash." And that's just what it was. Her birthday, June 19, is always a major event at the zoo, with reporters and TV crews on hand.

Keeping sea lions, seals, and even the occasional wal-

50

rus at a zoo as far from the ocean as Brookfield is not new. But keeping fully aquatic mammals like dolphins at an inland zoo seemed impossible thirty years ago. If you grew up in Chicago, you would have to travel to Florida or California to see these wonderful sea animals. Then, in 1961, Brookfield Zoo opened what it called Seven Seas Panorama, the first inland "dolphinarium." It was a revelation. Midwesterners flocked to see the bottlenosed dolphins perform. Other inland zoos imitated the Brookfield model.

In 1987, Brookfield Zoo opened a brand-new dolphin exhibit. The old one was beginning to wear out, and it was too expensive to repair. The new facility is more than three times the size of the old one. And much of the time, it's filled to capacity.

Brookfield Zoo is located just outside Chicago. The address is:

Brookfield Zoo
Brookfield, Illinois 60513

9

Snow Leopards

BRONX ZOO

Snow leopards and the Bronx Zoo are a good combination. The Bronx Zoo is in the running for the title "best zoo in the world," and snow leopards are in the running for the title "most beautiful animals in the world." Have you ever seen a snow leopard? If you have, you know they're elegant, graceful cats with long thick fur. Snow leopards' coats are marked with dark spots and rings and come in either a pale, creamy gray or a softly tinted yellow color. Snow leopards are well named. They live in the high, cold, snowy Himalayan Mountains of central Asia.

Snow leopards are big cats. Minus his tail, a snow

Snow leopard and cub
© *New York Zoological Society*

leopard is nearly four feet long. Add the tail, and you add three more feet of cat. Yes, the animal has a tail a full yard long.

Like so many other animals, the snow leopard is an endangered species. Rare in the wild, it's also rare in zoos. Snow leopards are solitary animals that roam over wide areas in the Himalayas following herds of goats,

Snow leopard and cubs.
© *New York Zoological Society*

sheep and deer. They hunt mainly at twilight or at night.

Snow leopards are hard to find in the wild, and even their habitat is hard to reach, which helps explain why there are so few in zoos. A few years ago, scientists from the Bronx Zoo set out to track the range and movement patterns of snow leopards in Nepal, a country high in the Himalayas. Mountain peaks, deep mountain canyons, and rushing rivers made it hard for the scientists to do their work. Not only did they have to fight the rough mountain terrain, but they had to cover many miles on foot before the winter snows arrived. Worse yet, there were very few trails. It was super tough going, but at last the scientists succeeded in radio-collaring snow leopards and learning a lot about them.

Thanks to the Bronx Zoo's snow leopard breeding program, you don't have to go mountain climbing in Nepal to see one. You can just go to the Bronx Zoo. Forty-eight snow leopard births have won the zoo the Edward H. Bean Award, which is given by the American Association of Zoological Parks and Aquariums in honor of the most important birth or hatching in a United States zoo.

The first snow leopard arrived at the Bronx Zoo in 1903, but not until the 1960s was a snow leopard born at the zoo. Since then, the zoo has sent snow leopards to zoos in Australia, Canada, England, Russia and Japan.

The Himalayan Highlands exhibit at the Bronx Zoo looks like a small version of the Himalayas. It has many of the plants, trees, and grasses that grow in the Himalayan region. Artists from Nepal have decorated the exhibit with hand-painted designs. Heat coils built into a rock allow snow leopards to bask in the sun, even on the coldest winter days. Snow leopards share the Himalaya Highlands exhibit with cranes and red pandas. Red pandas are not giant pandas. They look like big raccoons. Beyond the exhibit area are four quiet dens for snow leopard mothers and babies. There are also four hundred feet of interlocking runs.

Perhaps the friendliest snow leopard ever to live at the Bronx Zoo was Bowser. Bowser was the pet of an American Air Force pilot in the 1940s, during World War II. After the war, Bowser grew too big to remain a pet, and he moved into the Bronx Zoo. Bowser loved people so much he would purr whenever anyone came near. If a member of the zoo staff entered his cage, Bowser would get so excited he'd wrap himself around his visitor's feet and begin biting and scratching. It was friendly biting and scratching, but snow leopards are strong cats with sharp claws. Zoo staff members had to stop visiting Bowser inside his cage, but they could pat him safely through the cage bars.

A trip to the Bronx Zoo will give you a chance to see an enormous number of animals besides snow leopards. The zoo is the largest urban zoo in the United States, with well over 4,000 animals on exhibit. The Bronx Zoo has pioneered so many things it would take a book far larger than this just to list them. The zoo was a leader in zoo-dom from the day it opened in 1899.

Zoos all over the world have copied the Bronx Zoo's Children's Zoo, where kids can crawl through a prairie dog tunnel or climb a spider web. The Reptile House boasts a reptile nursery. There's a beautiful World of Birds exhibit and a very interesting Aquatic Bird House. Best of all may be the Jungleworld exhibit, where you can experience a tropical rain forest and see black leopards and giant water monitor lizards.

If you want to visit the Bronx Zoo, here is the address:

The Bronx Zoo
Fordham Road and the Bronx River Parkway
Bronx, New York 10460

10

White Alligators

AUDUBON PARK ZOO

Have you ever seen a white alligator? Probably not. They are among the rarest animals in the world. If you wanted to see some, you would have to visit the Louisiana Swamp Exhibit at the Audubon Park and Zoological Garden in New Orleans, an old zoo that has recently undergone major renovations.

These white alligators are New Orleans natives, or nearly so. They were found in a swamp southwest of New Orleans by fishermen on September 3, 1987. Four of them were brought to the zoo and put on exhibit in October. Nine more of the rare animals were left in the swamp, under the watchful eye of wildlife experts.

Baby white alligator
Courtesy Audubon Park and Zoological Society

Only one white alligator was previously known to exist. It is believed to have hatched from eggs laid by the same female as the current crop.

These white alligators are not albinos, that is, they don't completely lack dark color. They have white skin and dark eyes. True albinos would have pink eyes.

In the swamps and bayous of Louisiana, there have been lots of legends and tales about white alligators. They are usually associated with good luck. But we don't know if the people who told the stories had ever really seen a white alligator or if they simply made up the stories.

The true white alligators were found on property owned by the Louisiana Land and Exploration Company, an oil and gas company. The president of the company said that he certainly hoped all the legends about white 'gators were true. "They are supposed to appear before a period of prosperity. We are certainly ready for such a period in our industry," he said. The Louisiana oil and gas industry has been going through hard times over the last few years.

The white 'gators are expected to quickly outgrow the swamp exhibit. A special white alligator exhibit is being built for them. It is hoped that these unique animals will breed both in the zoo and in their protected place in the wild. Alligators are known to breed well in captivity. If they are left alone, they do very well in the wild, too.

Not too many years ago, it looked as if the American alligator would be hunted to extinction. Then, strict rules on hunting alligators were passed. Alligator populations throughout the South began to rise quickly. In some places, alligators have gone from being an endangered species to a common sight. 'Gators have been around since the time of the dinosaurs, so they are pretty tough.

The New Orleans Zoo isn't all swampland. It's a modern full-scale zoo, with exhibits of animals from around the world. A few years ago, another white animal became a superstar at the Audubon Park Zoo. She was Suri, the white tiger. The white tiger isn't an albino, either. It is a color variation of the ordinary Bengal tiger, as blond or brunette hair in humans is. The white tiger has ashy gray stripes on a white background. Its nose and paws are pink, and its eyes are ice blue. White tigers also tend to be a bit larger than ordinary Bengal tigers.

Suri the white tiger
Courtesy Audubon Park and Zoological Society

India has had legends about white tigers for hundreds of years. The tigers have always been considered lucky. For a long time, such tigers were thought to be only legends. Then, in 1951, a male white tiger was caught in the Rewa Forest in India. The tiger was named Mohan, the Indian word for enchanter.

Mohan lived in the palace of one of the princes of India. He lived a long time and fathered a large family. Many of his descendants were also white. Today, fifty-two white tigers are known to be living in zoos in different parts of the world.

Suri was born in the Cincinnati Zoo on August 19, 1982. She was loaned to the Audubon Park Zoo in 1983. She quickly became the star of the zoo. With Suri on exhibit, zoo attendance shot up 40 percent. She was supposed to be sent back to Cincinnati on November 1, 1983. But Suri was so popular that the Audubon Zoo asked to have her visit extended. And when the extension came to an end, the Audubon Park Zoo still couldn't bear to part with the beautiful animal. The Cincinnati Zoo was quite willing to sell Suri, but the price was high—$200,000. The Audubon Park Zoo went public. They asked for donations. The people of New Orleans responded quickly, and generously. The magnificent white tiger is now a permanent and very popular resident of the Audubon Park Zoo. You can go to see Suri at:

The Audubon Park Zoo
6500 Magazine Street
New Orleans, Louisiana 70118

11

Greater One-Horned Rhino

SAN FRANCISCO ZOO

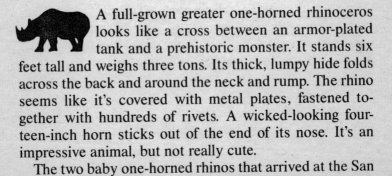 A full-grown greater one-horned rhinoceros looks like a cross between an armor-plated tank and a prehistoric monster. It stands six feet tall and weighs three tons. Its thick, lumpy hide folds across the back and around the neck and rump. The rhino seems like it's covered with metal plates, fastened together with hundreds of rivets. A wicked-looking fourteen-inch horn sticks out of the end of its nose. It's an impressive animal, but not really cute.

The two baby one-horned rhinos that arrived at the San Francisco Zoo in June 1987 were surprisingly cute. The thick hide was there. But at less than a year old, they had

Shanti and Chattra, the one-horned rhinos.
Photo by Anne Dowie. Courtesy San Francisco Zoological Society.

not yet developed a horn. All they had was a little lump on the nose. The rhino does not reach full size or have a fully developed horn until it's six to eight years old.

This pair of young rhinos were a gift of the king of the tiny country of Nepal. The female was named Shanti and the male Chettra. Taken together, the Nepalese names mean "zone of peace."

Shanti and Chettra were instant stars. The mayor of San Francisco was on hand to greet them. They got a large enclosure all to themselves. Rhinos look slow, but they aren't. They can run at twenty-five miles per hour, and they like to gallop around for exercise. They also have a big pool to soak in, another favorite rhino pastime. One-horned rhinos are excellent swimmers. As growing children, Shanti and Chettra must have plenty to eat. They each devour about fifteen pounds of apples, bananas, carrots and sweet potatoes a day, plus an eighth of a bale of alfalfa.

All rhinos have very small eyes and are pretty nearsighted. If something is more than one hundred feet away, they can't make it out very well. But they have a wonderful sense of smell. They can catch the scent of food a half mile away. They also have very good hearing. Watch a rhino closely, and you will see it swivel its ears around constantly.

The greater one-horned rhino is one of five species of rhinoceroses that lives in Asia or Africa. Practically everywhere in the world, the rhino population is declining, everywhere except Nepal. Nepal is a small and remote kingdom of mountains and jungles between China and India. Though Nepal is one of the poorest nations in the world, and its population is growing rapidly, it has been remarkably successful at conserving its wildlife, particularly the greater one-horned rhino. The rhino population of Nepal has jumped from a low point of 108 in 1970 to nearly 400 today. That's a real triumph.

The government of Nepal has been so successful at conserving rhinos that its main rhino reserve already has as many of the animals as it can handle. Nepal has estab-

The penguins at "Tuxedo Junction"
Brian Katcher photography. Courtesy San Francisco Zoological Society.

lished a second rhino colony. And some rhinos, like Shanti and Chettra, have been sent to zoos around the world.

There are now nine zoos in America that have one-horned rhinos. Rhinos breed pretty well in the zoo. These nine zoos have joined in a program to help ensure that these strange and wonderful animals will be around for future generations to marvel at.

While Shanti and Chettra were instant stars at the San Francisco Zoo, they had some competition. The zoo also has koalas, one of only three American zoos to display the engaging creatures.

The zoo is extremely proud of Tuxedo Junction, its large display of Magellanic penguins. These birds come from an island near the Strait of Magellan at the southern tip of South America. Fifty of these penguins were brought to San Francisco in May 1984. This particular type of penguin had rarely been kept in zoos before, so no one really knew what to expect. How did they do? Much better than anyone could have hoped. Four years after the colony was established, the population had nearly doubled.

There are lions and tigers and snakes and crocodiles at the San Francisco Zoo. But if you're really brave, you can visit the Insect Zoo—it's one of only three in the country. There, you can see hissing cockroaches and giant African millipedes. Zoo officials swear that their weekly "tarantula talks" are among the zoo's most popular programs.

If you want to visit the San Francisco Zoo, here is the address:

The San Francisco Zoological Society
Sloat Boulevard at the Pacific Ocean
San Francisco, California 94132

12

California Sea Otter

MONTEREY BAY AQUARIUM

Otters are just about the most charming animals in the world. You've probably seen otters frolicking around at the zoo. But the chances are that the sort of otters you have seen are river otters. They live in freshwater lakes and rivers all over the United States. They are fairly common. But there is another kind of otter, the sea otter, and you have probably never seen one of those in a zoo.

At one time, there were thousands of sea otters living off the coast of California. The sea otter has a wonderful thick coat, and it was hunted nearly to extinction for its fur. In 1911, there were only fifty California sea otters left. The government finally decided that something had to be done. All sea otter hunting was banned. Slowly, the otter population began to recover. Now, there are about 1,300 of these delightful animals cavorting off the California coast.

Sea otters did not do well in zoos, so most zoos simply didn't try to keep them, and still don't. If you want to see a California sea otter up close, you'll have to go to an area near where they live. In Monterey, California, is one of the newest animal exhibits in the world. The Monterey Bay Aquarium sea otter exhibit is unique, and it has only been open since October 1984.

The Monterey Bay Aquarium is the largest aquarium in the country, and practically all of the animals in it come from the region within a few miles of the exhibit itself. The area of Monterey Bay contains one of the richest varieties of sea life to be found anywhere in North America. In fact, if you stand on the terrace of the aquarium, and look out over the bay, you may be able to spot one of the types of animal that's also on display inside. The aquarium gives you a chance to get a really good look at these creatures.

There are sharks and rays and schools of anchovies. It's not just a collection of fish tanks. The exhibits display the sea creatures in completely realistic settings. There is, for example, a huge kelp forest exhibit. Kelps are varieties of giant seaweeds. Kelps the size of small trees sway gently inside a twenty-eight-foot-deep tank. Swimming in and around the kelps are hundreds of fish: silvery halfmoons, lavender surfperch, gray sand sharks, and silver jack-smelt. It's truly a scuba diver's view, but you don't have to get wet to see it.

Do you want to know what a starfish or a bat ray feels like? There is a shallow pool where visitors are encouraged to reach in and touch the creatures.

California sea otter.
© 1987 Monterey Bay Aquarium

But the unquestioned stars of this spectacular new facility are the sea otters. There are just four of them at the moment, though the aquarium hopes to establish a regular breeding colony. Each of these otters was found ill or abandoned when very young. They were carefully raised at the aquarium with the aid of volunteer otter sitters, who gave them 24-hour-a-day care.

The Monterey Bay Aquarium does more than exhibit otters. It serves as a sea otter center. Injured or sick otters are brought there. Sea otters are often the victims of oil spills, all too common on the California coast. The aquarium is one of the places where otters are brought to be cleaned and cared for. Most otters that are brought to the aquarium and recover are released back into the sea. The four that were completely raised by humans would not have been able to survive in the wild. That's why the aquarium kept them.

Sea otters are not easy or cheap to keep. The four Monterey Bay otters have an enormous 55,000-gallon tank to play in. It's good for the animals, and it's good for visitors. The top of the tank is open to the sky, and visitors can stand on the deck and watch the otters on the surface of the water. Or they can go downstairs and, through nine viewing windows, see the otters swimming underwater. Otters are friendly creatures that don't seem to mind all the attention. When they do want a bit of privacy, they can get it by swimming into an underwater rock grotto. It isn't really rock. Like many of the other features in the Monterey Bay Aquarium, the otter grotto is made of acrylic plastic. It's so realistic that neither the visitors nor the otters seem to know the difference, or if they do, they don't care.

Sea otters have huge appetites. They must eat at least 20 percent of their body weight every day. If an otter weighs fifty pounds—the average weight for a full-grown female sea otter—then she eats about ten pounds of food a day. The food—clams, crabs, squid and fish—isn't cheap, either. It costs about $10,000 a year to feed one California sea otter.

In the wild, sea otters rarely come to land. In the water, they are graceful swimmers. On land, they look clumsy. They eat while in the water, and the way they do it is one of the most stunning features of sea otter behavior. Sometimes, they will float on their backs and use their stom-

The "Touch Tide Pool," which allows visitors to touch various sea creatures.

achs as trays. They pick up food with their paws. Occasionally, a sea otter will put a flat rock on its stomach and crack clams against it while floating. This isn't necessary in the aquarium. There, the otters will crack clams against the windows of their tank, sometimes startling visitors.

There is a great deal that we still don't know about how sea otters behave. The aquarium hopes that its exhibit will not only delight visitors, but will also help scientists learn more about the lives of these wonderful animals.

The Monterey Bay Aquarium is housed in what used to be an old fish-canning factory, at the north end of a street called Cannery Row. There is a well-known novel called *Cannery Row,* written about the area. A movie has also been made from the book.

The once thriving fish-canning business began to close down in the 1950s. By 1971, the Hovden, largest of the canneries, was forced to shut its doors, and the whole area began to decline. But a small group of dedicated marine biologists, aided by a big grant from a computer millionaire (whose daughter happened to be one of the biologists), bought the Hovden factory. They have turned it into what is being hailed as one of the three or four best new aquarium buildings in the Western Hemisphere.

Since the Monterey Bay Aquarium opened, millions of visitors have flocked to see it and its star attractions, the playful California sea otters.

If you get a chance to visit the Monterey Bay Aquarium, don't miss it. The location is:

Monterey Bay Aquarium
886 Cannery Row
Monterey, California 93940

13

Sea Lion

MYSTIC MARINELIFE AQUARIUM

Even legends retire. In 1987, word spread throughout New England that Skipper the sea lion was finally calling it quits. Skipper had been the star attraction at Mystic Marinelife Aquarium in Mystic, Connecticut, for thirteen long years. During training demonstrations in the aquarium's amphitheater, his dazzling single-flipper stand brought waves of applause. Let the aquarium's bottlenose dolphins do triple spirals and back flips. Let the beluga whales cavort. Nobody upstaged Skipper in the amphitheater's 350,000-gallon center pool.

Despite his success, Skipper has had his share of ups

and downs. The ups came the day his trainer taught him to climb a ladder. As for downs, well, down is the only way to describe what happened when the ladder broke. The 570-pound Skipper went tumbling to the bottom. Luckily, he wasn't hurt, but he was certainly alarmed. So was his trainer. Both trainer and sea lion decided then and there that from now on there would be no more ladders in Skipper's act.

Audiences didn't care. Ladder or no ladder, Skipper was still a first-class acrobat. What's more, he had a knack for making human-like sounds. Whenever the blubbery beast came out with what seemed to be an "oh yeah," audiences cheered.

Though Skipper's farewell performance is a thing of the past, he has not said farewell to his fans. Nowadays, he leads a life of comfort and ease in the aquarium's Sea Island exhibit, where he's still a center-stage attraction. Once a superstar, always a superstar.

Skipper is legendary in more ways than one. He is the last California sea lion at the Mystic Marinelife Aquarium who was born in the wild. Mystic has had such great success breeding sea lions that the aquarium has no need to take them from the wild anymore. Sea lions are born in June, so if you visit the aquarium during the summer months, you'll be able to see the babies at their cute and playful best.

Even in the wild, a sea lion is an animal version of a stunt man. Sea lions have been known to leap out of the water and clear a hurdle seven feet high. They enjoy lining up and jumping dolphin style. Sometimes, they're so playful that they jump right over each other's backs. Young sea lions have a lot of fun chasing each other through the water, barking and honking.

Some people think a sea lion sounds more like a lion

Skipper the sea lion
Robert Patterson, The Day.

roaring than a dog barking. That's why the animal is called a sea lion. When you think about the games sea lions play naturally in the wild, it's not surprising that they easily learn to perform tricks when they live in zoos or circuses.

In circuses, sea lions are often billed as performing seals. But sea lions aren't seals. One way to tell the difference is to look at the animals' ears. Seals look as if they don't have ears. That's because seals don't have ear flaps. Ear flaps are the outer part of an animal's ears, the part that shows. If you want to see great ear flaps, take a look at a cocker spaniel. As for sea lions, they have small but noticeable ear flaps.

Another difference between seals and sea lions is the shape of their rear flippers. Sea lions can rotate their rear flippers forward beneath their bodies. Seals can't. This means that while seals are great swimmers they're not much use on land. Sea lions are great swimmers, too, but because of their rear flippers, they can move along on land.

How big is a sea lion? Males can reach a length of seven feet, while females can grow to six feet. Despite their large size, sea lions are sleek, muscular animals. They're fun to watch even when they're resting. Just look at their friendly faces and big, round, soft eyes, and you'll know why they're among the most appealing zoo animals in the world.

All sea animals tend to be big eaters. To keep its animals well fed and happy, the Mystic Marinelife Aquarium has a massive walk-in freezer that holds 60,000 pounds of fish. Another reason why animals at Mystic are lively and active is the facility itself. It's just plain super. Sea Island boasts diving ledges, a tide pool where baby animals can learn to swim in safety, areas where animals can haul themselves out of the water comfortably, and temperature-controlled freshwater pools.

What kind of hospital does the aquarium have? Why, one with a pool, of course. Sick animals are kept in a special saltwater pool at Mystic, and veterinarians are on staff to treat them. Speaking of salt water, Mystic is proud to have pioneered a special artificial sea-water mix that makes it possible to locate an aquarium anywhere, even inland. For years, aquariums had to be right on the ocean, because the only way to get salt water was directly from the sea.

Mystic is also proud of its animal rescue program. With the help of volunteers, the aquarium helps rescue sea animals stranded on New England beaches. The aquarium also runs many interesting programs on sea animals, including a two-and-a-half-hour study cruise for kids. There are lots of animals on display at the aquarium besides Skipper and the other sea lions. There are all kinds of fish including sharks—and even ducks and frogs.

If you want to visit the Mystic Marinelife Aquarium, here is the address:

Mystic Marinelife Aquarium
55 Coogan Boulevard
Mystic, Connecticut 06355

14

Prairie Dog

ARIZONA-SONORA DESERT MUSEUM

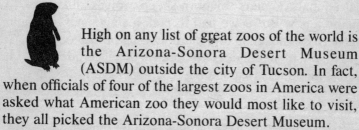

High on any list of great zoos of the world is the Arizona-Sonora Desert Museum (ASDM) outside the city of Tucson. In fact, when officials of four of the largest zoos in America were asked what American zoo they would most like to visit, they all picked the Arizona-Sonora Desert Museum.

It's called a museum, but with more than 200 different kinds of animals on display, it is at least part zoo. It's the animals that most visitors come to see, though there are also lots of plants and other exhibits. It is certainly a new style of zoo.

Merv Larson, ASDM director, says, "The staff is largely made up of people who have an interest in natural history, some talent for building things and who want to experiment with finding ways to communicate their ideas and feelings about natural history. We try to display and describe certain features of this particular region."

The ASDM was first opened in 1952. It now has more than 16,000 loyal members, who contribute generously of their time and money to make it a success. And it surely has been that.

The animals are shown in settings that are as naturalistic as possible. Zoo experts agree that no other zoo in the world does it better. Since the ASDM is located out in the desert and limits itself to animals of the region, it has a somewhat easier task than a city zoo trying to display lions in a naturalistic setting. But still, the accomplishments of this small museum-zoo are impressive. Many of the display techniques have been eagerly copied by other larger zoos throughout the world.

In a sense, the real star of the Arizona-Sonora Desert Museum is the place itself. Still, there are plenty of popular animals, jaguars, bighorn sheep, wolves and bears, to name a few. But if we had to pick a single star, it would have to be the small and plain-looking prairie dog.

No, it isn't a real dog. The prairie dog is a rodent, and it looks like one. Most of all, it resembles a tan squirrel with a short tail. It was called a dog because it makes a barking noise when frightened.

The prairie dog lives in underground burrows and tunnels. At one time, the prairie dog ranged across most of the prairie states. Hundreds of millions of the little rodents would gather in vast "prairie dog towns." Their tunnels and burrows would extend over hundreds of square miles. But ranchers and farmers moved in, and while there still are prairie dogs around, their numbers have been greatly reduced, and the vast towns no longer

Prairie dog
Photo Gill Kinney. Courtesy of the Arizona-Sonora Desert Museum.

exist. Prairie dogs now live mainly in national parks. But at ASDM, the visitor gets a chance to see the prairie dog up close.

The prairie dogs are constantly rearranging the burrows in the little town at ASDM. A prairie dog burrow has several entrances, so that if one is blocked, there is always another way in or out. Each burrow entrance is surrounded by a mound of packed soil. The prairie dog packs the soil down by hitting it with his head. The raised area is a lookout post and also acts as protection against flash floods after heavy rains.

The prairie dogs of the ASDM are pretty safe from floods. Coyotes are not likely to enter the enclosure, either. But there might be danger from birds of prey. The ASDM is so completely part of its surrounding environment that wild animals often wander into it. Sometimes, it's hard to tell where nature leaves off and the man-made exhibits begin.

While prairie dogs spend a lot of their time underground, digging or cleaning tunnels with their long claws, they also spend time at the entrance to the burrow watching out for predators. As soon as one is spotted, they give a sharp bark, and dive back into the hole. The bark alerts all the other prairie dogs, who do the same.

Life in a prairie dog town, or in this case a prairie dog exhibit, is never simple. Each family has its own definite territory. Family members defend their territory from intrusions by members of other families. Prairie dogs rarely fight seriously. When they want to warn off an intruder, they will stand up on their hind legs, point their nose in the air, and make noises. Usually, the stranger retreats. Occasionally, there will be a squabble, but no one gets seriously hurt.

The prairie dog isn't the sort of animal that you will see in most zoos. Or if one is there, it is so ordinary looking that you might not even notice. But in this unique desert zoo, you can see them under conditions that are as close to natural as possible. And that makes them special.

The Desert Museum is located fourteen miles from downtown Tucson, Arizona. The address is:

Arizona-Sonora Desert Museum
2021 North Kinney Road
Tucson, Arizona 85743

15
Walrus
THE NEW YORK AQUARIUM

New York City is famous for having lots of everything. But there's one thing the Big Apple has only one of. A walrus. The walrus's name is Nuka, and she lives in the New York Aquarium in Brooklyn. There are two kinds of walruses, Atlantic and Pacific. They are very much alike. Nuka is a Pacific walrus. If you go to see her, you'll find her in the aquarium's Tripool exhibit, where she shares a pool with a female sea lion named Breezy. If she's not there, look for her in the aquarium's Aquatheater. Nuka puts on quite a show. The large animal is such a big crowd pleaser she outshines even the electrifying electric eel.

Nuka the walrus
Photo by Valerie Hodgson. Courtesy the New York Aquarium.

Very few zoos or aquariums have walruses. Why? To begin with, look at where the animals live. Walruses almost never move south of the Arctic Circle. Even to see a walrus in the wild, you have to undertake a major journey. When you find a walrus, you won't find it living by itself. Walruses live in herds of up to a hundred animals. It's very hard to lure a walrus away from his herd.

But even getting hold of a walrus or two doesn't solve the problem. The animals do not travel well, and it's a long way from the Arctic Circle to a zoo.

Even if a walrus makes it to a zoo safely, he won't be easy to keep there. A male walrus can weigh as much as 3,000 pounds, and a female walrus can easily weigh a ton. That's a lot less than an elephant weighs, but elephants eat hay. Walruses eat fish, and fish is expensive. What's more, despite his vast size, a walrus's stomach holds only a gallon of food. So walruses have to keep eating and eating and eating. A male walrus named Olaf who lived in the New York Aquarium in the sixties used to consume 140 pounds of fish a day! A zoo could go bankrupt trying to keep a walrus well fed.

The New York Aquarium is able to keep walruses because it's one of the largest, best equipped, and most

Beluga whale
Photo by Valerie Hodgson. Courtesy the New York Aquarium.

important aquariums in the world. More than 20,000 sea creatures, rare and otherwise, live at the Aquarium—including the Pacific octopus, the toadfish, piranhas, clownfishes, sea turtles and penguins.

Walruses are wonderful. You'll know it the minute you see one. An adult walrus has a thick, hairless, blubbery body. The palms and soles of his flippers are bare, rough and warty. He makes loud bellowing noises and elephantlike trumpeting sounds. A moustache with hundreds of stiff bristles sprouts from his face. A male walrus's tusks can be a full yard long, and each tusk may weigh as much as eleven pounds.

Watch a walrus a while, and perhaps his odd appearance will begin to make sense to you. Blubber helps keep a walrus warm. Bellowing and trumpeting alert other walruses to danger. In the wild, a walrus's tusks are useful for dredging up shellfish from the bottom of the ocean. Tusks also help a walrus get a good grip on the ice, so he can haul himself out of the water. The moustache? A walrus uses it to help shovel food into his mouth.

In zoos, walruses are basically amiable creatures. Olaf was pushed around so badly by a pair of elephant seals that the seals had to be removed from his pool. At the Bronx Zoo, a walrus named Herbert was so playful he kept trying to hug the harbor seals that shared his pool. In the wild, crowds of walruses sunbathe together on sheets of ice. Sometimes, the ice gets so crowded that the sheet tips, and the walruses fall into the sea.

Falling into the water is no problem for a walrus. A walrus's flippers are well adapted both for swimming and for getting around on ice or land. Walruses can move with surprising speed out of water. Once heavily hunted for their tusks, walruses sometimes played turnabout and chased their hunters across the ice.

Don't pass up the chance to see a walrus. Nuka and the New York Aquarium are waiting for you. The aquarium has a children's cove exhibit, where you can hold a living seastar, touch corals and sponges, and even explore a sand dune. Stop by the blue lobster exhibit. Blue lobsters are so rare they occur only once in 30,000,000 times! Go see the aquarium's shark tank.

The aquarium offers lots of exciting programs for kids. You can have breakfast with the animals. First, you feed them. Then, you feed yourself. Study gulls on the Coney Island beach. You can even hold your birthday party at the aquarium. The aquarium has a holding facility for the care and rescue of stranded animals. Next door to the aquarium is a major research center called the Osborn Laboratories of Marine Sciences.

The New York Aquarium opened in 1896, and since then it has seen a lot of firsts. It was the first aquarium to exhibit beluga whales. The first beluga whale bred outside the wild was born there. The first demonstration of an electric eel lighting up a neon tube occurred at the New York Aquarium. Know what? The great New York Aquarium will go right on doing great things.

If you want to visit the New York Aquarium, here is the address:

The New York Aquarium
West 8th Street and Surf Avenue
Brooklyn, New York 11224

About the Authors

DANIEL COHEN is the author of more than a hundred books for young readers and adults. SUSAN COHEN is the author of several gothic novels and mysteries. The Cohens have coauthored a wide range of books for children and teenagers including *Heroes of the Challenger, Rock Video Superstars I* and *II, Wrestling Superstars I* and *II, Young and Famous: Sports' Newest Superstars,* and *Going for the Gold,* all of which are available in Archway Paperback editions.

Daniel Cohen is a former managing editor of *Science Digest* magazine and has a degree in journalism from the University of Illinois. Susan Cohen holds a master's degree in social work from Adelphi University. Both grew up in Chicago, where they married, later moving to New York. Today they live in Port Jervis, New York.